Three Years and Eight Months

Written by Icy Smith

Illustrated by Jennifer Kindert

East West Discovery Press

Manhattan Beach, California

Published by:
East West Discovery Press
P.O. Box 3585, Manhattan Beach, CA 90266
Phone: 310-545-3730, Fax: 310-545-3731
Website: www.eastwestdiscovery.com

Written by Icy Smith
Illustrated by Jennifer Kindert
Design and production by Icy Smith and Jennifer Thomas

Photo credits:
Pages 40–44 — Japanese troops enter Hong Kong, © Imperial War Museums (HU 2766); British prisoners of war marching to captivity in Hong Kong, © Imperial War Museums (HU 2779); The Union Jack is raised at Stanley Civil Internment Camp in Hong Kong, © Imperial War Museums (A 30506); Japanese soldiers prepare to march to a prisoner of war camp, © Imperial War Museums (SE 5146); Japanese war criminals prepare for their transfer to Stanley Jail, © Imperial War Museums (SE 5156); Page 42 — Japanese military notes, courtesy of Icy Smith; Page 43 — 26th Fighter Squadron in front of Flying Tigers P-40s, courtesy of Gene O. Chan; Page 44 — Yu Choi Tang in front of the Supreme Court Building, courtesy of Kwan Chi Lam.

Library of Congress Cataloging-in-Publication Data

Smith, Icy.
  Three years and eight months / written by Icy Smith ; illustrated by Jennifer Kindert.
    p. cm.
  Summary: Recounts the Japanese occupation of Hong Kong from 1942-1945 as Choi, a ten-year-old Chinese American boy, secretly joins the resistance and saves thousands of American, British and Canadian forces. Includes historical notes and photographs.
  Includes bibliographical references (p.)
  ISBN 978-0-9856237-8-4 (hardcover : alk. paper) 1. China--History--1937-1945--Juvenile fiction. [1. Hong Kong (China)--History--Siege, 1941--Fiction. 2. China--History--1937-1945--Fiction. 3. World War, 1939-1945--China--Fiction. 4. Spies--Fiction.] I. Kindert, Jennifer C., ill. II. Title.
  PZ7.S64927Thr 2013
  [Fic]--dc23
                              2012040668

ISBN-13: 978-0-9856237-8-4 Hardcover
Printed in China
Published in the United States of America

This book is dedicated to my father, uncle, and grandmother, who lived the reality of Hong Kong during the Japanese occupation. My uncle was forced to work for the Japanese military and transported prisoners to death camps. As a result, he suffered serious posttraumatic stress disorder. My father was a slave boy who witnessed the Japanese brutalities and is still coping with emotional healing. My grandmother was victimized by Japanese soldiers for three long years and became a nun after the end of World War II.

— I.S.

*For Tim Yun Arnstad Kindert,
my beloved nephew and source of inspiration.*

— J.K.

Acknowledgments

My deepest appreciation to the following individuals who made this book possible:

Mr. Kan Siu Ping and Mr. Gary Mok
of the Chinese Alliance for Commemoration of the Sino-Japanese War Victims,
for their research and loyal support;

Mr. Ng Yat Hing and members of the Hong Kong Reparation Association,
for sharing their agonizing memories of life during the Japanese Occupation;

Bill Lake and Tony Banham, for their invaluable expertise and advice on military history;

Gene O. Chan, for his photo permission on Flying Tigers;

my families in Hong Kong and California, for their love and encouragement;

and last but not least, my husband, Michael, for his extraordinary unceasing support.

— I.S.

My special thanks and gratitude to the following persons
for their generous help and support:

Michael Li; Linda Li; David Li; Ahnry Avina; Minh Quach;
Joshua Lam; Mike Schneider; Jenney Chang; Irwin Tang;
Lisa Schmidt; Cheryl Collett; Philomena Jones; Rossi Walter

— J.K.

My dad passed away when I was little. My name is Choi. Mom, Uncle Kim, and I live in a rundown apartment building in crowded Hong Kong. Today, on my way to school, something strange occurs, with loud sirens and smoke in the distance. It doesn't sound like the usual drill of the British soldiers.

When I get to the school's auditorium where we always meet in the mornings, teachers, parents, and students are running around frantically. The school principal makes an announcement: "Japanese planes are bombing Hong Kong. Everyone must go home now." Shells whistle through the air, then loud booms echo through the streets.

The journey back home feels like a thousand miles. I see some Japanese soldiers break
into shops and search the apartments above them. They are very cruel, and they rob
people, too. They set up roadblocks and shoot at people. The Japanese soldiers are
taking some young men and women away. I'm scared and want to be at home with
Mom and Uncle Kim, but roadblocks block my way. I pass through winding alleys
until I see Uncle Kim. We both are gasping for breath, and Uncle holds my hand tight.

When we get near home, we see Japanese soldiers dragging people out of their homes. Mom is one of them! Uncle Kim and I hide behind a wall with our fists clenched, but we are afraid to be taken away, too. I can't take it any longer and run to Mom and grab her arm, shouting, "Mom, don't leave!"

She bursts into tears. "Choi, don't worry about me! I will be back soon. Listen to Uncle Kim." A soldier pulls me away and pushes me hard to the ground with his gun pointing at me. They let me go; perhaps because I am only a 10-year-old boy.

8

Uncle Kim shudders with rage, and I cry. After the soldiers leave, he explains that Japan invaded China a few years ago and is now taking Hong Kong. Japan also launched a surprise bombing in Pearl Harbor, an American naval base in Hawaii. Now, the United States and Britain are fighting Germany and Japan.

Uncle Kim says, "Choi, we are at war with Japan now and need to work together to save Hong Kong." He holds me tight and whispers, "We will find your mom and everything will be all right." I lose my voice crying myself to sleep.

On Christmas Day of 1941, Hong Kong surrenders to Japan. It is known as "Black Christmas." In the following months, we hear that many villages have been burnt down. Businesses close down, food becomes scarce, and thousands of people are starving. Many die from starvation, and many disappear. Mr. Chan, our neighbor, along with other young men, is forced to work as a slave on remote islands. Girls are taken away, too. I see young women, including my music teacher, Ms. Lee, covering their faces with dirt and disguising themselves as men. They are afraid to be taken away by the Japanese army.

Japanese soldiers carrying rifles with bayonets patrol the streets. When we see the soldiers on the street, we must bow to them. One day, I saw a man being beaten by a soldier for not bowing to him. We even have to bow to the Japanese flag.

Each family is rationed small amounts of rice, oil, salt, and sugar every month. And every month, we go to a food station and wait in line for half a day for our small portion of food.

No one eats more than one small meal a day. Most of the food and medical supplies are kept for the Japanese troops. We hear that some of our food supplies are being shipped to Japan. Every family has to turn in all their valuables, including Hong Kong money, in exchange for Japanese military notes. If citizens are found with Hong Kong money, they are punished. Some are even killed. People live in fear even if they obey all the rules.

This morning, my uncle, his friend Aaron, and I hike up the mountain to collect firewood. The cute monkeys playing on the way make me laugh—the first smiles we have had in months. Uncle Kim tells me to go look for wood. Aaron's son Taylor and I do that, while Uncle and Aaron talk about something important.

It is my first time meeting Taylor. I know his mom is an American. He looks a little different from us, with lighter eyes and skin. He can speak both Chinese and English.

"Where is your mom, Taylor?" I ask.

"She went to the United States to visit family in California before Japan attacked Pearl Harbor. Now that we are at war, she can't come back," Taylor replies. I think of my mom a lot and wonder if I will ever see her again.

Our arms are full with wood, and we go to the soldier station to trade it for a small loaf of bread. Unlike the other soldiers, one is quite friendly to Taylor and me. When the other soldiers are not around, he teaches us some Japanese words. His name is Watanabe-san.

A year passes, and Japanese soldiers stop distributing food. People are now eating tree bark, leaves, and roots. We manage to find some potato flour to eat, but many people are hungry or dying from hunger. Taylor, Uncle Kim, and I are staying alive by trading firewood for food with Watanabe-san.

Many people sell clothing and the few belongings they still have to street vendors in exchange for food. One day, thousands loot the Japanese warehouses and try to steal back food supplies. Many are caught and never seen again. Life is horrible in Hong Kong.

Watanabe-san and I have become good friends by now. He tells Taylor and me that we have learned enough Japanese to work at the military station. We will be slave boys, but at least we will get some food. The soldiers trust kids more than adults.

The next day, I give a big farewell hug to Uncle. He looks at me with a solemn face and says, "I'll come to see you every week. Since you can understand Japanese quite well now, maybe you can find out information for our people. You might be able to help end the war." I'm shocked to hear this, and wonder if I'm really able to help.

19

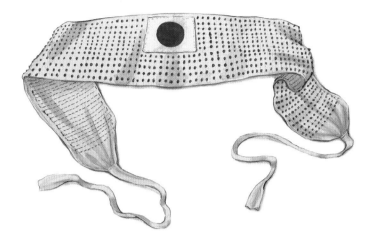

Watanabe-san says Taylor and I will have Japanese names from now on. I'm called Tooto-san, meaning "little brother." Taylor, who is older than me, is called Nii-chan, meaning "older brother."

Watanabe-san shows us around the rooms and offices in the station where we will work. There are a few desks in each room, and each desk has a radio and other interesting machines. Watanabe-san explains that soldiers listen to announcements on the radios and use the machines to type out what they hear. The machines are called typewriters. "Your job is to keep all rooms and bathrooms clean and to deliver packages to different military stations."

Taylor and I learn more about Japanese culture when Watanabe-san has free time. We learn to sing Japanese songs and the national anthem, and we learn Japanese manners.

Over the months, we have shown the soldiers that we are good workers. One day, Taylor is asked to deliver a package to another building. Taylor comes back looking uncomfortable and says, "I just saw many women working in a building a few miles from us. And I recognized my classmate's mother there. Some are washing clothes. Some are sewing. Others are folding and packing uniforms. They all look sad and don't talk to each other. When I pass by some rooms, I hear women sobbing. It is eerie. Maybe your mom is working in there, too." I am appalled to hear about the women's living conditions there, and I wonder if what Taylor said is true.

24

The next day, I ask Watanabe-san if I can deliver packages, too. I run to the same building Taylor visited, in hopes of finding Mom. All around the courtyard, women are working in bad conditions, washing clothes by hand with wooden scrubbing boards. Suddenly I spot my mom! I recognize her right away, because she is still wearing the same blue blouse she wore the day she was taken away by the Japanese soldiers.

"Mom!" I yell as tears start running down my face. She turns around and is stunned, but happy, to see me. "Oh, Choi, I'm so glad you're still alive," Mom speaks with a muffled voice to keep the soldiers from hearing. She cries silently while holding me tight.

"What are you doing here?" Mom asks with a wistful look on her face.

"I learned to speak some Japanese and now work and live at the Japanese military station. I am making a delivery today and maybe I can come here again. One of the soldiers treats me well and gives me leftover rice soup," I explain. "What about you, Mom? How have you been doing here?"

"I am okay, but we must work hard without breaks. This is a bad place."

I look up and see a soldier grabbing a woman by the wrist and dragging her inside.

"We are not allowed to leave the building or talk to anyone outside here," Mom whispers. "If the soldiers see us talking, we may be taken away to work on a remote island. You must go, but we can smile at each other if you can come by again."

We see a soldier walking toward us. Mom signals me to go. As I leave, the stern-faced soldier asks, "What are you doing here?" My heart beats and says, "Delivering this parcel." "Then get on with it," he shouts.

I tell Taylor what happened. "I am glad that you found your mom," Taylor says, beaming. "This will be our secret. No one will ever know."

That night, Uncle Kim comes to see Taylor and me. And I tell him about my mom.

He is ecstatic to know his sister is safe. But Uncle Kim has a disturbed look on his face.

"What's wrong, Uncle Kim?" I ask.

"I see many dying and injured people every day. I wish I could help. If I only had medical supplies…" Uncle Kim sighs.

"I know where some medical supplies are stored in the station," I reply.

"No, it's far too risky for you," Uncle Kim says with a trembling voice.

"I want to help my people. Please let me try," I convince Uncle Kim.

Uncle Kim pauses, then after a few minutes he nods his head and says slowly, "Yes, please be careful."

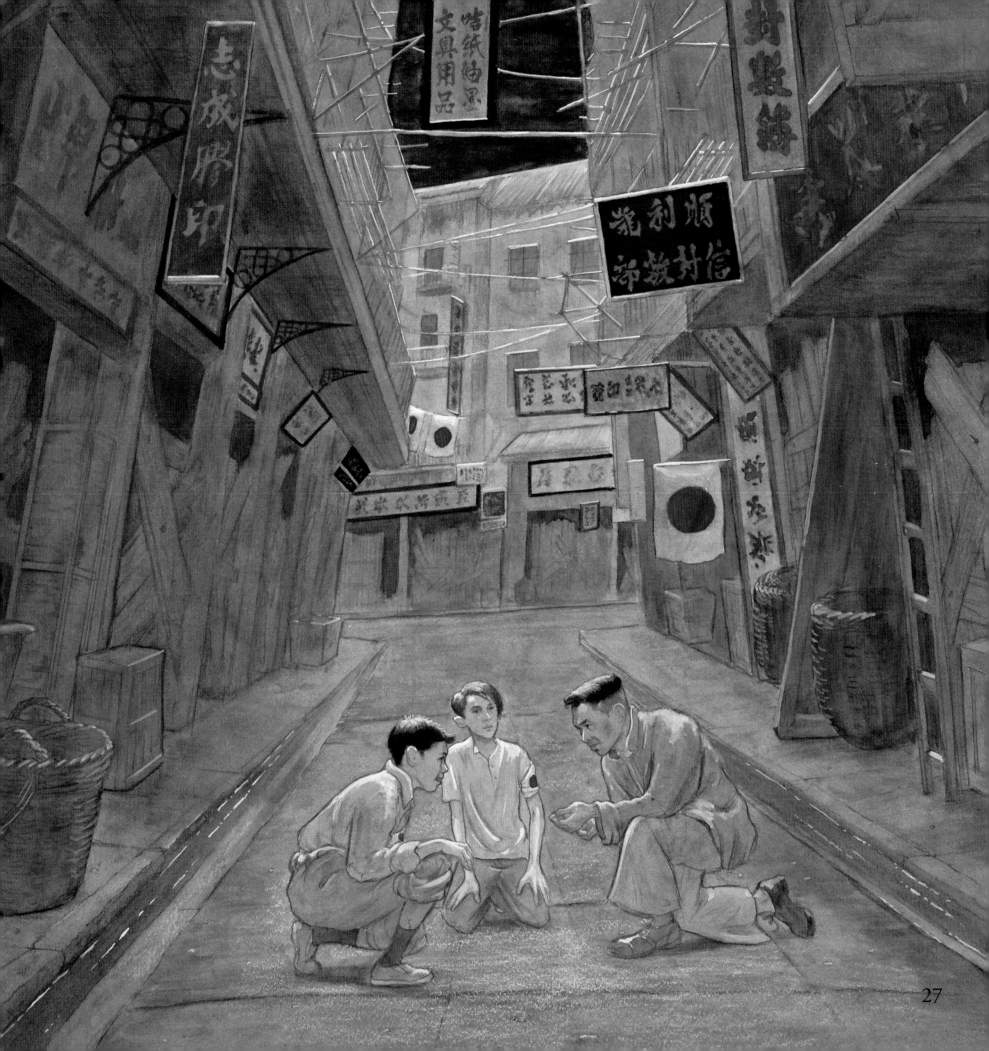

In the following months, I get to see Mom when I deliver parcels to her building. She looks more exhausted, but seeing me always brings a smile to her face. Taylor and I find the medical supplies in the storage area. Every few days, we each secretly take a few items and put them in a hideout area where Uncle Kim can come at night and retrieve them.

One night while we are hiding some supplies, we hear footsteps and see a shadow near us. Taylor immediately grabs my wrist and motions me to stop. Our hearts pound until the shadow disappears. For many months, we are able to get the much-needed medicine for Uncle Kim.

One day as we are getting the supplies from the storage room, a soldier walks in. "What are you doing here?" he asks, furious. We look at him with terror and do not know what to say, but Taylor leans back and then says, "I cut my arm and want to get a bandage." Taylor shows a bloody cut on his arm to the soldier. The soldier looks at us and says, "These supplies are for Japanese only!" And then he leaves.

"Wow, that was a close one. How did you do that?" I ask.

"I just leaned back on the sharp edge of the drawer and cut myself." Taylor flashes me an impish smile. I'm surprised by Taylor's quick thinking and bravery. I'm proud of him.

Two years pass by, and times get even tougher. We have managed to continue pilfering medical supplies, and no one has noticed anything missing. One day, many soldiers gather in the room where Taylor and I are cleaning the floor. They cram together and listen to a radio announcement in English from the United States. One soldier is translating the English to Japanese on a piece of paper. Since Taylor knows English, he can understand. But he pretends he doesn't understand as he cleans the floor in front of the soldiers. I look at Taylor and ask, "What is happening?"

"The United States has dropped an atomic bomb on Hiroshima, Japan. Thousands of Japanese have died. The United States called for a surrender of Japan," Taylor whispers to me in Chinese.

We see the fury in the Japanese soldiers' eyes and know they are upset. Watanabe-san has a solemn face and glances at us.

Uncle Kim comes to see us, and we talk about the news. Uncle Kim has a big grin on his face and says that this means the war will soon be over. He finally tells us his role during the war years.

"Taylor's dad and I belong to an underground anti-Japanese resistance group called the East River Column. We have been fighting the Japanese troops and destroying their weapons and supply lines. We also help our Allied prisoners of war escape as well as rescue Allied American and British pilots who were shot down by the Japanese. The medical supplies you have been providing us were for the injured resistance members and prisoners. You two have saved hundreds of lives. Our group has more important work to do tonight. The American and British forces may continue to bomb, so you two must be very careful. We'll meet again soon."

In the next few days, when no one is in the radio room, Taylor and I go inside to see if we can find more news. On the bulletin board, there is an urgent announcement in Japanese. We learn that the United States dropped another atomic bomb on Nagasaki, Japan. All of a sudden, a shadow appears. It is Watanabe-san.

"Leave the room quickly before you are caught by other soldiers," he whispers in a croaky voice. At that moment, we both realize that the shadow we saw before when hiding the supplies was Watanabe-san. He knew about our rescue effort all that time.

The American and British warplanes continue to bomb the Japanese transportation lines and warehouses outside of town. Some drop parachutes of food and medicine into the prisoner camps where thousands of Allied and Chinese prisoners of war have been incarcerated.

On August 14, 1945, Japan surrenders unconditionally. It was the American, British, and Chinese Nationalist Army forces working together that liberated Hong Kong.

Watanabe-san tells us that he and the other soldiers will be relocated to internment camps and hopefully return to Japan soon. "The station is now closed. Both of you should go home," he says.

Taylor and I are sad about his leaving, as he has been kind to us. He is one of the few Japanese soldiers who has shown humanity and helped their enemies at war. Watanabe-san looks down and says, "Soldiers will not be welcome back home in Japan after losing in a war." We tearfully say goodbye to each other. And we never see him again.

People are extremely relieved that the atrocities committed by the Japanese army have come to an end. "We should go find your mom," Taylor suggests.

When we arrive at Mom's building, we see hundreds of women leaving. Many of them have lost their families and homes during the war. Many feel shame for socializing with Japanese soldiers and end up becoming Buddhist nuns.

Mom is safe, and when I see her this time, I run to her and hold her tight. We know the nightmare has ended finally, after three years and eight months.

Taylor misses his mom so much and presses his lips to hold back from crying. Mom invites Taylor and his dad to live with us as they wait for news from America.

Soon, Taylor receives a letter back from his mom.

Dear Son,

I'm very proud of you and your friend Choi's bravery and contribution to the war resistance group. By risking your own lives, both of you have done heroic deeds for justice. With your help, many American, British, Canadian, and Chinese prisoners were saved from their injuries and helped to escape. I have received permission from the U.S. government for you to immigrate to California. I will patiently wait for you and your dad to arrive.

Love,
Mom

Taylor is stunned by this news. He is happy to know he will soon see his mom again. But at the same time, he is sad to leave me. Although we will be thousands of miles apart, we promise to write letters to each other to maintain our brotherhood.

Remembering History

Fall of Hong Kong

Within moments of the infamous attack on Pearl Harbor in the U.S. by the Japanese Imperial Army, another surprise bombing took place in Hong Kong, a former British colony. On Dec. 7, 1941 (Dec. 8 in Asia), Hong Kong began its darkest period of history: a brutal Japanese occupation lasting three years and eight months.

The devastation began at the Kai Tak Airfield, Sham Shui Po Barracks, and residential areas in Kowloon. After 18 days of bloody fighting by the British, Indian, and Canadian forces against the overwhelming Japanese army, Hong Kong suffered great loss of life including 1,500 defenders. The Japanese army looted homes, burned villages, and assaulted and killed thousands of civilians. To celebrate their victory, the Japanese soldiers were given implicit permission for three days to rob, rape, and kill anyone in Hong Kong.

Japanese troops enter Hong Kong led by Lieutenant General Takashi Sakai and Vice Admiral Miimi Massichi.

The governor of Hong Kong, Sir Mark Young, surrendered control of Hong Kong to Japan at the Peninsula Hotel in Kowloon on Christmas Day of Dec. 25, 1941—the day the Hong Kong people call "Black Christmas." On Feb. 20, 1942, General Rensuke Isogai became the first Japanese governor of Hong Kong.

St. Stephen's College Massacre

Shortly after the Japanese invasion, the School House of St. Stephen's College was turned into an emergency military hospital by the Hong Kong government. On Christmas Day, 1941, 150 to 200 Japanese troops broke into the School House. Doctors and nurses stepped forward to surrender and were shot or bayoneted where they stood. The troops killed 56 British and Canadian soldiers who were still wounded helplessly in their beds, as well as some medical and college staff. Seven nurses were raped and eyewitnesses documented acts of unspeakable brutality. This atrocity is known as the "St. Stephen's College Massacre." During the Japanese occupation, the School House was turned into an internment camp. About 1,000 internees were housed in St. Stephen's College.

Prisoners of War

The Allied prisoners of war (POWs) suffered atrocities during the Japanese occupation. Following the surrender of Hong Kong, approximately 9,000 allied POWs, mostly British, were detained in various internment camps in North Point, Sham Shui Po, Argyle Street, and Ma Tau Chung. Some

British prisoners of war marching to captivity in Hong Kong.

2,700 British, American, and Dutch civilians were confined in the Stanley Internment Camp. Detainees suffered severe malnutrition and many were tortured. Thousands were shipped to Japan as slave laborers in factories and coal mines and thousands more died from hunger, diseases, and execution. Less than half of the original POWs survived through to the end of the war.

Food Rationing

As there was inadequate food supply, firewood, and medicine, many people died from starvation and diseases. The Japanese military government rationed necessities such as rice, oil, flour, salt, and sugar. Each family was given a rationing permit, and every person was given 6.4 taels (8.5 oz.) of rice per day. Most people did not have enough food to eat, and many died of hunger. The rationing system was canceled in April of 1944, as limited food supplies were shipped to the Japanese military bases in the Pacific. People survived on potato powder, peanut powder, wild plants, tree bark, and rats. Some even resorted to cannibalism. Life was terrifying.

Forced Repatriation and Massacre

Japanese forces mandated unemployed people to return to Mainland China. Many were sent to Hainan Island as laborers. They were forced to work for long hours and were left unattended when sick. Eyewitnesses reported that the Japanese soldiers would randomly pick up truckloads of people on the streets and drop them off in boats. Forced into the open sea, they were then killed by machine guns. Some fishing boats were set on fire. Many were murdered by the Japanese soldiers simply because they were considered unpleasing to their eyes. As a result, the Hong Kong population dropped from 1.6 million before the war to less than 600,000 in 1945.

Military Note

The Japanese outlawed the Hong Kong currency and replaced it with the Japanese military note. Hong Kong people were forced to exchange their Hong Kong dollars, gold, and other precious metals for Japanese military notes. The initial exchange rate was two Hong Kong dollars to one military yen in January 1942. Later it went to a four-to-one ratio by July 1942. The Japanese military note was made the sole legal tender in June of 1943. Anyone who was found possessing the Hong Kong currency would be tortured or even executed. In September 1945, the Japanese troops were evacuated from Hong Kong, without giving Hong Kong people the opportunity to exchange the money back to anything of value. The Japanese military yen became worthless. Most Hong Kong people went bankrupt overnight.

Education

Starting in May 1942, some schools were reopened with mandated Japanese language classes to instill Japanese culture and values into Hong Kong people. Students were required to learn Japanese for at least four hours a day. Japanese became the official language. In addition, all main street names and buildings in Central District were renamed in Japanese. For example, Queen's Road Central became Meiji-dori, and Des Voeux Road became Shōwa-dori. Buildings such as the Gloucester Hotel became the Matsubara; and the Peninsula Hotel, the Matsumoto.

Anti-Japanese Resistance

Formed in 1939 by the Communist Party of China, the East River Column was mostly comprised of peasants, students, and fishermen. When the war reached Hong Kong in 1941, the guerilla force grew from 200 to more than 6,000. The anti-Japanese guerrillas' most significant contribution to the Allies was their rescue of 20 American pilots who parachuted into Kowloon when their planes were shot down by the Japanese.

On February 11, 1944, six bombers and 20 fighter aircrafts from the American 14th Air Force, including the 32nd Fighter Squadron of the Chinese American Composite Wing (CACW), bombed the storage area at Kai Tak Airfield, Hong Kong. Two American pilots were shot down on the mission. They were Lieutenants Yang Y. C. and Donald Kerr, both from the 32nd Fighter Squadron, CACW. Yang was killed, but Kerr was rescued and escorted by members of East River Column through thousands of miles crossing enemy lines. He was finally handed over to the British Army Aid Group (BAAG) in Huizhou, China, six weeks after he was shot down.

There were an estimated 38 American Air Force personnel rescued by the Chinese guerillas from 1942 to 1945. The Column was a distinguished force in South China.

The Hong Kong-Kowloon Brigade was established in February 1942, later renamed the Hong Kong-Kowloon Independent Brigade under the command of the East River Column. They were armed with machine guns and several hundred rifles left by the defeated British forces. By mid-1943, the Brigade had nearly 5,000 soldiers and operated in Sai Kung. It played an active role in fighting the Japanese both on land and at sea, often in conjunction with the Allied troops.

Japanese Military Notes

26th Fighter Squadron of the 5th Fighter Group in front of Flying Tigers P-40s, 1944

The Brigade was also well-known for its rescue effort of intellectuals and prisoners of war. Lieutenant-Colonel Sir Lindsay Ride, founder of the BAAG along with many British and Chinese military officers, were rescued and escaped to China shortly after the Japanese invasion.

American 14th Air Force – Flying Tigers

The first American Volunteer Group of the Chinese Air Force known as the famous "Flying Tigers" was created in 1941 to combat Japanese forces in Hong Kong, China, and Burma. Later, in 1943, it became part of the 14th Air Force comprised mostly of Chinese Americans with Commander Claire Lee Chennault. Working closely with Allied forces, they trained Chinese Air Force ground crews, performed troop transport, repaired planes, and participated in notable aerial battles against Japan Army Air Force. Toward the end of World War II, they dropped parachutes of food and medicine into the internment camps and helped liberate Hong Kong. The Flying Tigers played an important role in defeating Japan in Hong Kong and South East Asia.

British Army Aid Group (BAAG)

Impressed by the bravery and the discipline of the Chinese guerillas, Lieutenant-Colonel Sir Lindsay Ride founded an underground organization called the British Army Aid Group (BAAG) in southern China. Its mission was to assist the escape of POWs and shot down Allied airmen in Hong Kong and China. Later, with the cooperative effort of the Allied Chinese and American forces, it became involved in gathering intelligence, providing medicines to the injured POWs, and distributing war news throughout the internment camps.

Japanese Surrender

The Japanese occupation of Hong Kong ended after the United States dropped atomic bombs on Hiroshima and Nagasaki on Aug. 6 and 9, 1945, respectively. More than 94,000 Japanese were killed. Japan surrendered unconditionally on Aug. 15. Admiral Sir Cecil Harcourt commanded a fleet of 24 Royal Navy ships and entered Hong Kong harbor on Aug. 30, to take surrender of the Japanese. The British control over Hong Kong was restored on Sept. 1. Admiral Harcourt was appointed commander-in-chief and head of the military government of Hong Kong, and accepted the formal Japanese surrender in a ceremony on Sept. 16, 1945.

The Union Jack is raised at Stanley Civil Internment Camp, Hong Kong, watched by the internees.

Japanese naval and marine personnel, having been confined to their barracks at Kowloon since the landing of British forces, prepare to march to a prisoner of war camp.

The author's father, Yu Choi Tang, was a slave boy for the Japanese military. He stands in front of the Supreme Court Building that was taken over by the Japanese troops and became "the headquarters of the Hong Kong Military Police" during World War II in Hong Kong.

Japanese War Tribunal

The Japanese military ruled Hong Kong with brutality and terror. During the Japanese occupation, an estimated 100,000 civilians were killed with countless inhuman acts documented.

General Sakai was executed on Sept. 30, 1945. Nineteen senior officers were hanged. And many were given prison sentences, including the Japanese governor, General Rensuke Isogai.

Reparation Settlement

During the Japanese occupation, the Japanese military government had issued 1.9 billion military yen. Today, there are 540 million military yen in the hands of the 3,500 members of the Reparation Association Hong Kong (RAHK). The RAHK has appealed to the Japanese government for reparation since 1993. However, the Japanese government has rejected their claims citing the 1951 San Francisco Treaty between the British and Japanese governments.

Japanese war criminals prepare for their transfer to Stanley Jail, Hong Kong.

The RAHK filed an appeal to the High Court because the Treaty of San Francisco was signed between the British and Japanese governments, but not the Hong Kong citizens. And the treaty had no mention of the Japanese military notes. Although each note states "legal tender," the issue has yet to be resolved. An appeal of the reparation settlement is still in process.

Acknowledging the Past

To date, successive Japanese governments have to some extent been in denial of the atrocities committed by the Japanese soldiers in Hong Kong during World War II. Some have publicly proclaimed that these events were fabricated. And worse, some modern Japanese textbooks have bias and omissions regarding the brutal acts of Japanese soldiers. Many Japanese students remain unaware of their own history.

It is hoped that the history of *Three Years and Eight Months* will never be forgotten: "Those who cannot remember the past are condemned to repeat it" (George Santayana).

WORLD WAR II JAPANESE OCCUPATION, 1942

CHINA

JAPAN

HIROSHIMA
NAGASAKI

HONG KONG

U.S.A.

HAWAII

PEARL HARBOR

PACIFIC OCEAN

 OCCUPIED BY JAPAN